D0494669

THE BOOK OF
MINI-SAGAS II

THE BOOK OF MINI-SAGAS II

from the

TELEGRAPH
SUNDAY MAGAZINE

competition

ALAN SUTTON
1988

ALAN SUTTON PUBLISHING
BRUNSWICK ROAD · GLOUCESTER

First published 1988

Copyright © Telegraph
Sunday Magazine 1988

All rights reserved. No part of this publication
may be reproduced, stored in a retrieval
system, or transmitted, in any form or by any
means, electronic, mechanical, photocopying,
recording or otherwise, without the prior
permission of the publishers and copyright
holder.

British Library Cataloguing in Publication
Data

The Book of mini-sagas II
1. Short stories, English
2. English fiction—20th century
823'.01'08 [FS]   PR1309.S5

ISBN 0-86299-486-1

Typesetting and origination by
Alan Sutton Publishing Limited
Photoset Garamond 12/12
Printed in Great Britain by
The Guernsey Press Company Limited
Guernsey, Channel Islands

PREFACE

Yes, there is an art of the mini-saga, as our entrants testify. The attraction of the mini-saga, a story of exactly fifty words, neither more nor less, has now challenged readers of the *Telegraph Sunday Magazine* on three occasions, and has on each occasion elicited an extraordinary number of responses.

What we look for when judging the competitions is a mini-saga that tells a story. We prefer it not to be an anecdote, although often the anecdotes have merit enough to win a prize. One anecdote that does not win is a recycled joke. We received a lot of those.

Also, I think a mini-saga should have some dimension to it: time should pass. It should have gravity. That's to say, it should make a point which has some drama or psychological truth. It must aim, in fact, to be a saga in miniature. Here's an example, called *The Hero*:

Yellow banners came down from the mountains. Triumphant soldiery poured into the capital. Everywhere, cheering citizens, waving flags, music.
Their rebel leader, the national hero, appeared on the *rathaus* steps.
'This day marks a new epoch in the history of our land,' he shouted.
So began twenty years of tyranny.

Judging mini-saga competitions is a pleasure. We hope contestants also find enjoyment battling against too many words. Congratulations and thanks to all who entered, and who feature in these pages. Literacy is alive and well and living in the *Telegraph Sunday Magazine*. Each paragraph here contains exactly fifty words, incidentally.

BRIAN ALDISS

CONTENTS

INTRODUCTION

Judging a mini-saga competition is an epic undertaking. It demands mighty concentration, aeons of time to spare, a knowledge of history, warfare, myth and religion – and an heroic appetite for lunch. All five judges of the *Telegraph Sunday Magazine*'s 1987 mini-saga competition fulfilled these criteria admirably. The only time their brave resolution foundered was in reaching some consensus about the winners. Which should give much comfort to those of you – readers and writers alike – who could not decide whether the restrictions of the fiendish, fifty word format constituted a serious narrative form, or a joke. If it's any help, the judges didn't know either.

This time our band of pioneers comprised: Brian Aldiss, novelist and sci-fi writer; Alan Coren, humorist and editor of *The Listener*; Felicity Lawrence, editor of the *Telegraph Sunday Magazine*; Brian Redhead, presenter of BBC Radio 4's 'Today' programme; and Heidi Thomas, whose playwriting career was launched when she herself won a competition – Texaco's 1984 'Most Promising Young Writer' award. Each was asked to explain, pithily and wittily of course, how they compiled their shortlist of best entries, many of which are printed on the following pages.

Said Felicity Lawrence:

'I was looking for something that caught my attention immediately. The best of them told a story and left a lasting emotional impression, or else offered new insight. I cannot pretend I was looking for an heroic form, nor was I too worried about Aristotlian principles of a beginning, a middle and end. A saga which is mini is such a contradiction anyway that it seemed more important that the form was humorous than anything else. But the winner had to be something more than just a cryptic joke. In too many cases you could tell from the first line that the words were building up to a joke you had heard before.

'People tended not to develop titles properly – when you came across an instance where the title actually added to the text, that was a bonus. Some of the most powerful mini-sagas came from the children. Their naïvety suggested that the experiences they described were personal and gave their efforts greater intensity.'

Said Brian Redhead:

'To me, there is a real difference between a mini-saga and an incident. If a story is just a fifty word description of something that happened, no matter how comical or neatly turned, that is not a saga. A good saga not only has a beginning, a middle and an end, it is part of a bigger experience and should leave you with the feeling that there is more to come. I also liked a bit of splendour and majesty – a saga that says something big and important, but says it very simply.

'I was not looking for big words, only right ones. With a limitation of fifty words, you shouldn't really find any adjectives. And if you put an adverb in, it is usually because you have chosen the wrong verb. For me, a mini-saga also has to have a measure or rhythm – not necessarily a rhyme, though with our winner, we plonked for that too. Ideally I like reading them aloud to myself, partly because you want them to sound alright on radio, but also because you should feel that the words are coming out in the right places. It's part of the old oral tradition.

'I love the idea of the fifteen word title because it is exactly the opposite of the mini-saga itself. In fifty words you have to encompass something quite majestic; whereas in fifteen words you are being asked to create a gigantic tease. Not enough people made anything of the opportunities in the title.

'The first sentence of a mini-saga should make you sit up – as in good journalism, which grabs people immediately and gets them thinking, "I want to know more". I also feel a mini-saga should be memorable, so that when you have read it a couple of times, you are able to remember it. And an element of parable is quite important as in *The Virus* which I liked very much and which had a slightly moralising tone.

'The fifty words ought to be a distillation, though you do have to be careful not to turn the idea into a calculated exercise, like some huge crossword puzzle.'

Said Heidi Thomas:

'I was looking for economy of language combined with epic statement. Just because the format was short didn't mean that the subject matter had to be trivial. Every word should carry weight. And if by dint of ambi-

11

guity, one word could be made to do the work of two, I was especially interested. Irony and pun I found attractive, but I didn't like those that were no more than a build-up to, or a feed for, a final punch line.

'I also looked for metre, or an innate rhythm to the piece. I think a mini-saga is in effect a poem, so in order to convey the maximum amount of information in the minimum number of words, you do have to use language in a non-naturalistic manner.

'As I am a sentimental person, anything with love in it was a winner. I liked ideas that aroused my emotions, as in *What God has joined together – man can put asunder*, which didn't win but made the shortlist. However during the judging, I remember admiring something as being 'poignant' and being loudly decried by the three men.

'The children's themes astounded me. I expected work that was more imaginative and less responsible, but they were all astonishingly aware of the burden of the twentieth century. On the one hand it depressed me – on the other, I felt they must have great belief in their potential as adults because they produced a great awareness of real values. I am thinking in this instance of the winner of the Under-18 category, *Out of the mouths of babes?* and *Invincible*, a runner-up.'

Said Alan Coren:

'Our criteria for judging was very elastic, which made the whole process very difficult. Redhead required the entries to fulfil the description of saga and be rather Norse in flavour. I was looking for ingenuity within the circumscription of fifty words. And for humour.

'The very word 'mini-saga' is comic. So a mock-epic form, rather like a limerick was OK by me. However, there *was* a lot of stuff about dogs falling in love . . . the main fault of entries was sentimentality linked to sententiousness, plus sloppiness and self-indulgence. If a thing is short and pithy, there is a danger it will become pompous or po-faced.

'The children were a bit glum but it would be an enormous mistake to extrapolate from that and think, "Kids today are glummer than we were." Kids always do bang on about death a bit. I think this is due to adolescence, when they are confronted with the idea of immortality and instead of dealing with it, they tackle mortality.

'Being the sort of journalist who likes to run off at the mouth a bit, getting anything into fifty words that approached a story filled me with admiration. I gave plus points for anything extra – like being in verse, or comic, or having an original line. The winner, *Strange Eventful Hairstory*, fulfilled all my requirements.'

Pat Garratt
Telegraph Sunday Magazine

SUNG HEROES

STRANGE EVENTFUL HAIRSTORY

Hirsute Sweeney bound his
hair
And killed the dragon in its
lair.
He passed through ice and fires
of hell,
Freed the princess from her
spell,
But then released the locks he
cherished
And in a cloud of dandruff
perished.
Thus heroes resolute and
imperious
May die of nothing
serious.

Prof. P. Brockbank

STRATFORD-UPON-AVON

— *1ST PRIZE – ADULT* —

HALF A LEAGUE,
HALF A LEAGUE,
HALF A LEAGUE
ONWARD

They were tough men. They had
  come this far together.
Overcome many hazards. Now,
  wolves threatened them.
They must move forward – fight
them. Nerves frayed, they broke
cover. Into the open where the
  wolves waited. Battle was
  tough, two men injured.
Triumphantly they won.
  Next week they must
    face Arsenal.

Nancy Calladine

SPONDON

INVINCIBLE

He will not live, they said.
He is now thirty-one.
He will not walk, they said.
He ran the London Marathon.
He will not be independent,
they said.
He owns a flat in town.
He'll be a loser all his life, they
said.
He beat them all,
hands down.

Jane Grinaway

FAREHAM

Age 14

— *RUNNER UP – UNDER 18* —

CHOCOLATE DESPAIR

Beautiful Freda,
hair blowing, stood at the top.
The sheer rock face,
unclimbed by man below.
He starts to climb,
hot with crampons and pack.
Many tortuous hours pass.
He reaches the top.
She runs towards him,
arms outstretched.
Glancing over the edge,
the Milk Tray is at the bottom.

Robert Games

GLOUCESTER

Under 18

REMEMBRANCE DAY

My husband comes
from a proud military
tradition. His grandfather
fell at Gallipoli, honoured
for selfless gallantry. His
father was among the heroic
paratroopers who died at
Arnhem. Our son was killed at
a football match, stabbed by a
rival fan. He was wearing a
white poppy at the time.

Margaret Staunton

CAMBERLEY

THE HERO

Yellow banners came down from
the mountains. Triumphant
soldiery poured into the capital
city. Everywhere, cheering
citizens, waving flags. Their
great rebel leader, their hero,
appeared on the *rathaus* steps.
'This day marks a new epoch in
the history of our nation,' he
shouted. So began twenty years
of tyranny.

Brian Aldiss

— *COMMISSIONED EXAMPLE* —

WHO DARES WINS

He was scared.
It was his first drop.
The transport shuddered
violently on its journey
through the night.
They were over the
dropping-zone. Soon it would be
knives into unsuspecting bodies.
Killing silently.
'Ready?' said the Sergeant. 'Go.'
He said a prayer and jumped
into the streets
of Troy.

Rev. N.M. Cooper ·

NEATH

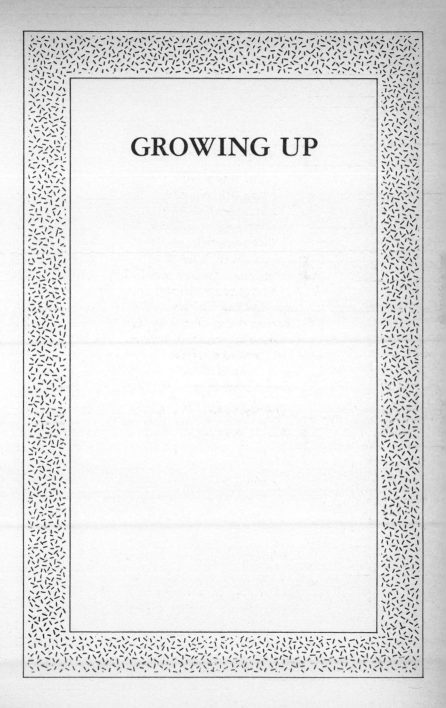

GROWING UP

FIRST LIGHT

'How
cramped
in here! I
elbow room, and
hear a crack, a
crunch. How warm and
snug. But what is this
white that breaks my
comfortable darkness.
Wriggle, tap: Oh! my
home, shattered: light
piercing, cold
invading.
And here
I am naked
and wet.
Fragments of
eggshell all about me.'

John Paul Evans

TELSCOMBE CLIFFS

A NANNY'S NIGHTMARE

Two snotty,
spotty monsters appear,
flicking cereal across the table.
Painting today.
I return from lunch.
They've painted. Their rooms!
Faces! Clothes!! Typical!
Once cleaned they're shown
to their parents.
The angels, they cried.
I leave my angels with their
tails and horns well hidden,
and plastic halos polished.
ANGELS?

A.G. Seager

BURTON-ON-TRENT

Under 18

IN A MINUTE DARLING, MUMMY'S BUSY

'You didn't come
to the school play!'
'Sorry, Mummy had to go
to her "Encounter Group".'
'Why didn't you come to my
Graduation Ceremony?'
'It was a vital meeting
of the Greenham Common
Committee.'
'Your mother is ill.'
'Sorry Dad, but I've just
consulted my Filofax and I'm
fully booked.'

Kathleen Golding

BANSTEAD

BACK AND FORTH

A middle-aged
couple playing tennis,
parted at the net, not married,
not divorced but separated.
Although they leave,
the net remains between them
and their child bounces back
and forth like the ball
on the court.
They may be happier apart but
the ball has to absorb the
punishment.

Lisa Nixon

COLCHESTER

Age 12

— *RUNNER UP* – *UNDER 18* —

GROWING UP

I see myself growing up
in this world of ours.
This world where people
kill each other because their skin
is a different colour.
Where people murder and rape
others for no reason
or kill themselves
through drugs and alcohol.
Do I really want to grow up
in this world?

Christopher Wright

NORWICH

Under 18

AN EARLY MORNING WALK

I rise early
and throw open my window.
The dew is still wet on the
grass. I leave the house.
My dog and I run up the path
leading to the wood
and go wild.
Returning,
the people I meet smile
for they remember being young.
The freedom of childhood.

Jo Harvey

WESTERHAM

Age 13

THAT FORTIETH
BIRTHDAY FEELING

At twenty he grieved the loss of
his teens. At thirty the end of
his youth. He then crammed in
as many hectic exotic holidays as
he could afford.
On the day it rained. For the
first time he noticed white
clouds in the clear puddles
along the old road.

J. D. Birtwistle

DIDSBURY

RELATIVE VALUES

Mrs Newgood cared.
She cared for the Earth,
the welfare of its peoples
and its wildlife. She fought
to ban the Bomb, nuclear
power, acid rain, meat eating,
smoking and any alcohol but
wine. She cared for
Mr Everight who espoused
her causes. Her husband
was left holding the baby.

Michael Brightley

SHREWSBURY

ALL THAT MAY BE NECESSARY FOR A FULFILLED LIFESTYLE (THOUGH NOT FOR YOU OR ME)

Her parents gave
her a strand of pearls:
she outgrew them. Her husband
gave her a home and jewels: she
mislaid those. Her children gave
her pain, then love and pain:
she tired of that.
People give her a wide berth:
unkempt but content, she
gives stray cats shelter
unstintingly.

F. M. Joyner

CHANDLERS FORD

A MODEL LIFE THAT SHOULD HAVE BEEN THE LIFE OF A MODEL

Be good for your mummy, they
said. She was. And please your
daddy. She did. Learn for your
teacher. Ditto. Love your
husband. Duty done. Care for
your children, see to your
seniles. She died, expecting to
hear: How she bore with us!
Instead: how she bored us,
they sighed.

C. Andrew

ASHTON-UNDER-LYNE

PERSPECTIVE

Silence, pain, fear, comfort,
warm milk and smothering
breast. The first dry nappy, the
first caught ball, the first at
Oxford. Orgasm, love, delusion,
a neat wife who could say yes,
an untidy mistress who never
says no. Gold beaches, gold
watches, golden memories,
a little fear, soft pain,
silence.

I. M. MacDonald

BARDON MILL

DOMESTIC
DRAMAS

RICH BUT STILL HUNGRY

I had a chicken.
Daily it laid an egg
for my breakfast until one
day it started laying golden
eggs and so I was hungry every
morning getting thinner and
thinner. Until I thought to
sell the golden eggs to
a jeweller and buy
bacon and eggs
from the
shop.

Emmeline Child

DAVENTRY

Age 7

THE MAN WHO GOT
HIS LIPS BURNED

Young Miss Smith
was as nice as pie.
Sugar on top, promise of
yielding sweetness within. But
when the greedy young banker
tried to have her after one steak,
medium-rare, the chips and
mange touts, the rather
good red, he found
he'd bitten off
more than he
could
chew.

Jane Bukowski

TUNBRIDGE WELLS

SHARP PRACTICE

He was the centre of attention.
The sharp knife gleamed in the
candle glow. Glancing up he
saw five faces looking expectant
watching every mood.
Facing him lay the body – legs
pointing towards him. Deftly
he wielded the knife. They
admired his professionalism.
'Ready for serving'
was the roast chicken.

Desmond Bailey

SALTDEAN

SATURDAY SHOPPING

Home at last, light the gas fire,
fill the kettle. All that planning
had paid off. Silly women acting
on impulse always got caught.
Not her. Life would be different
now, have some meaning. The
bundle in the holdall stirred.
Rock it gently. 'Ssssh little love,
you are mine now . . .'

Diana Rigg

— COMMISSIONED EXAMPLE —

A NAMELESS FATE

Sitting, watching,
goggling at the box.
His legs begin to shrink.
His bottom grows fatter and
fatter filling the armchair he sits
in, slowly at first, then faster
and faster. His eyes grow square
instead of round.
His head slowly turns to jelly
from sitting in front
of the telly.

Abigail Woodman

DOVERCOURT

Age 11

DYING?

Thrown in with a crowd,
the door slams shut.
I hear water.
I feel redness oozing from me
colouring the water.
Gasping for air,
blood runs to my toes.
Knocked out by arms and legs,
I come round
hanging on the washing line —
a red sock
among pale pink laundry.

Lucy Ogbourne

WELLS

Age 11

HAIR'S BREADTH

Depressed, he entered the
hairdresser's salon. She towered
over him divinely, her red nails
descending to the scalp,
caressing the hair follicles.
Soothed, out gushed his troubles
until his soul was as naked as
his scalp. His adored goddess
smiled, took his money,
and went to strip
another man's hair.

Rob Shearman

HORLEY

Under 18

DO IT YOURSELF

It was impossible.
She snarled when he ripped
the fireplace out. She raved
when he built an indoor
barbeque. She screamed when
he burst the water main,
plumbing the jacuzzi. But he
noted with satisfaction she did
not even whimper when he
plunged the screwdriver
accurately deep into
her heart.

L. Coleman

KNUTSFORD

THE 10p PIECE

I lie
in the bottom
of a pocket, amongst
bus tickets and sweet papers,
turned by a hand, tossed in the
air. Dropped, rolling along the
ground, 'Clink!' I lie still
neglected by straying eyes.
I think about the warm
pocket where I could
be instead of
this cold
drain.

Jo Richardson

COLCHESTER

Age 12

BOILED OR FRIED?

First
I crushed the
enamelled walls, I
then peeled the shattered
pieces off, I scooped out
the silken flesh which balanced
on the coolness of the spoon,
I dug again this time to
reveal the splendid centre,
it was almost as if I was a
thief now stealing
precious gold.

Monica Lopez

LONDON

Age 12

A PAINFUL EXPERIENCE

I longed to get rid
of him for weeks. At last
I had the chance. I climbed the
stairs, cautiously entered
the room and in the mirror I
saw him grinning.
The door slammed,
a cry of agony,
it was over.
Wreathed in blood my tooth
dangled on the string.

Stuart James

BIRMINGHAM

Age 13

LIFE OR DEATH?

My back and thighs and legs
all ached from pain.
Every minute someone would sit
on me or push me away when
I was not wanted. I only
relaxed when a bell sounded
and even then it was only
for a few minutes
before someone
would sit on me again.

Celia Harborow

ST SAVIOUR

Age 12

THE TERRORS OF HOUSEWORK

Everything
was positioned, ready for action.
The button was punched —
an empty 'CLICK'
then the destruction began.
Terror reigned.
The area soon lay blighted.
Victims were taken every
second. Devastation, destruction
and that horrifying,
earth-shattering noise
that filled all space.
Suddenly,
the hoover was unplugged.
It was all over.

Elizabeth Hayward

COLCHESTER

Age 13

CONSTANCY

He had compulsions but never
told anybody except his wife.
He checked taps, switches,
doors, constantly. Things
became worse.
At last his
wife thought him
an embarrassment.
She organised a useful
compulsion. He must go
into hospital.
She then had to check taps,
switches and doors, constantly.
She joined him.

John K. Bettancy
ROWLANDS GILL

49

THE MISSION

As he ran he could see his
destination ahead, its dark form
loomed forbiddingly. Seeing the
time, he increased his speed. He
hurtled across the road, dodging
the traffic. Looking up, he saw
the door slowly closing. He
stopped it, wedging himself
in the gap.
'A loaf of bread, please.'

Caroline Wake

ELY

Under 18

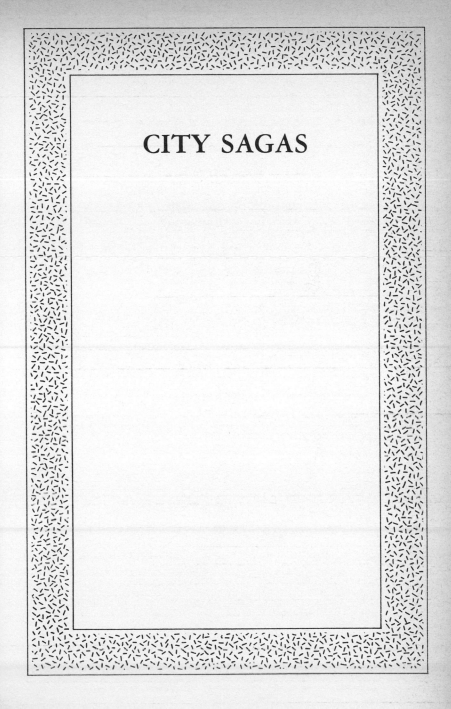

CITY SAGAS

THE COLLAPSE

They showed
pictures of the Stock Exchange
and told of its collapse.
His life savings gone.
Provisions for their future
up in smoke.
His dreams lay on the stock
market floor with the piles of
ticker-tape. His wife,
tea cup at her lips, said
'I wonder who cleans up.'

Ray Marshall

CHESTERFIELD

52

RICHES

The overnight news was bad.
As the day wore on the story
from the stock markets was the
same: down, down, down.
Billions of pounds were wiped
off the value of shares.
But it was the evening news
that impoverished us. The voice
of a cello had been silenced too.

Nicholas Hodgson

LONDON

THE NEW CHAIRMAN

'Goodbye Charles. No hard
feelings. Ten years was long
enough for me. I lasted by
attacking the strengths of any
possible rivals. Weaknesses are
obvious. Remember when I
called you a softie?
Get Baines to bring the car
round, will you.'
'Baines was sacked this
morning. Use the back lift.'

G. B. Turner .

NOTTINGHAM

MODERN CINDERELLA

Rupert Lombard parked his Porsche car carelessly that morning outside the stock market. Inside his flickering green-eyed fairy godmother told him that his paper dreams had been turned into paper disaster. That night on returning to the street he found a clamped pumpkin in place of his beloved Porsche.

C. R. Mitchell

SUTTON

THE FREE LUNCH

The Bank Manager sat at his desk. His thoughts drifted to yesterday. Bill had treated him to lunch. Chicken tikka, prawn biryani, two bottles of Chablis. Superb. The telephone interrupted his reverie. 'Hello, it's Bill here. Am I alright for another £10,000 on the company account for a few weeks?'

Martin Reece

KIBWORTH BEAUCHAMP

INSIDER DEALER

The noose tightening was
eternity.
Baker remembered everything:
breaching confidence, covert
deals and laundered money.
A champagne lifestyle was
severed by the policeman's
knock, then scandal preceding
the trial.
The judges verdict:
'. . . an example to others . . .'
Now, gnawing despair.
Sun through the cell window
formed a rainbow in his tears.

Gerald Friel

TRIMLEY ST MARY

EXCUSE ME, YOU ARE STANDING ON MY DIGNITY

'Bank charges
are a dishonest imposition,'
I said acidly.
Coolly indignant I faced
the Manager.
'Sorry,' I said with great
dignity, taking the cheque
with which the manager had, at
my insistence, closed the
account.
'Sorry,' I repeated, standing
up ready to leave.
I was still wearing my bicycle
clips . . .

D. J. Wood

LOWESTOFT

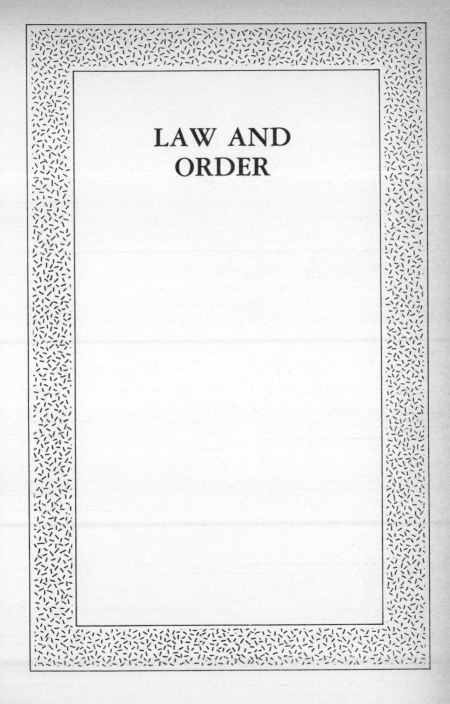

LAW AND ORDER

THE LAW IS BLACK AND WHITE

Black didn't think. White was
bloodied and beaten. A white
queen dying. Black, silently
crying, saw and understood.
White smiles grateful thanks.
Black, comforting, dresses her
indignity.
White knights turned a corner,
saw and understood. Called up
artillery. Black didn't think . . .
too late.
"But Baas . . ." was all black
ever said.

Steve Tranmer

H M PRISON
FEATHERSTONE

THE HOUSE OF LOOE CORNER

Sebastian Ayres,
notorious throughout Cornwall
as the 'Hood' for his evil
lidded eyes, growled impatiently
as young Christopher delayed
their night of felony by kneeling
at the feet of his lovely bride.
She spoke, innocent but gently
rebuking . . .
'Hush, Hush,
Mister Hood Ayres,
Chris, afore robbin',
is sayin' his prayers.'

Canon Kenyon E. Wright
Gen. Secretary Scottish Churches
Council

DUNBLANE

NOT A SENTENCE BUT A PARAGRAPH

The prisoner had committed
a very serious offence. His
barrister made an impassioned
plea on his client's behalf and
asked that the sentence to be
passed should be counted in
months rather than in years.
The judge listened patiently
and he acceded. He passed
a sentence of 48 months.

H. M. Scharf

SOLIHULL

BREAKAWAY

He left them screaming. The
crane swung, grabbed and lifted
debris. He sprang and clung.
The shots went wide. He
dropped, leaping free of falling
rocks and ran. Shades, bleached
hair and contact lenses saw him
through Customs. Won him
freedom. Imprisoned now in
alien heat he pined for
Pentonville.

G. Owen

LONDON

TIT FOR TAT

Skint. Benny and Trevor
boarded the bus intending to
give false names and addresses.
Finding their shillings, Benny
refused to share with Trevor.
'We've no money sir.'
The conductor takes out note
book.
'What's your names?'
'John Smith. . . .' lied Benny.
'And yours?'
'Mine sir. Is Benny. . .,'
squealed Trevor, suppressing
laughter.

James Daly

H.M. PRISON
GARTREE

THE YEAR THAT WAS

RAIN AID

It is raining here
but it isn't in Africa.
The people are hungry.
Some of the childrens' Mummies
and Daddies have died.
And the children are dying too.
I hope that it doesn't happen to
us. I sent Tee Shirts to Africa,
I wish I could send the rain too.

Rhian Lee

WANTAGE

Age 7

— 2ND PRIZE – UNDER 18 —

THE ADDICT

I had seen the television
commercials and read the
warnings but they were for weak
people, not for a strong person
like me. Besides, one try out of
curiosity would do no harm. I
must stop now. Fifty words
is all I can manage. My hands
are shaking
too much.

J. Halpin

GRANTHAM

THE TUNNEL

The British burrowed from the North, the French from the South. They met beneath the Channel and the necessary final adjustment was really quite small. Unfortunately, the additional stress it caused was critical and the party everyone was having in the middle to celebrate its construction was a complete washout.

Charles Hope

EXETER

DEEP SEARCH

It was that time of year,
so again they gathered at the
same place. Smoothly they
moved through the water.
Everything was noted; vibrating
sounds, shadows, shapes,
anything that would give a clue.
They reached the far shore and
looked to their leader —
'There's definitely something up
there,' said Nessie.

Kenneth R. Cox

ELTHAM

THE AIRPORT BUILDING AT ASSAB, ETHIOPIA, THE PORT WHERE THE GRAIN COMES IN

Leaning soldiers point casual
kalashnikovs. Hot winds scour
the arid runway and waiting
fifteen-seater. Security men
delve, frisk, interrogate Peter
Tyler, grain storage expert.
'Passport, permit, what are
these?' Prods his insect-infested
wheat samples. On an idyllic
poster, the slogan 'Ethiopian
Airways, going to great lengths
to please'.

Peter Crossley

SHEFFORD

VIRUS

And Rachel knew Anthony,
George, Matthew, Timothy,
Lawrence, Edward and James.
And Anthony knew Rachel,
Suzanne, Harriet, Alice, Judith,
Elizabeth, David and Ruth.
And so it came to pass that
by these couplings,
David slew James although he
knew him not, but doubtless
would have loved him
if he had.

Christopher North

LITTLE CHALFONT

THE SHUTTLE

We
sat down
to watch the
television
commentary
on the shuttle
going up.
'Hello, here
we are at Cape
Kennedy where
the space shuttle
is taking off.
And here it goes.
Its boosters are
going like mad
and it's up.'
'It's brilliant mum,'
said John. Sure is John.
It's brilliant.

James Moss

WATFORD

Age 10

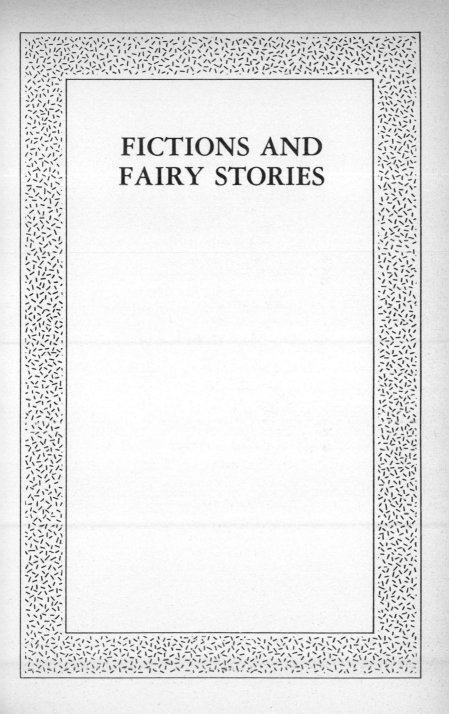

FICTIONS AND
FAIRY STORIES

THE ULTRA SOAP OPERA

Lavender Morny shook
her ringlets.
'I won't marry Bristow,'
she fumed.
'Yardley is nicer.'
Her father withdrew her
allowance, and mother schemed.
That evening, Andrew Cussons
met her in the pub. 'Let's
elope,' he whispered in her
fascinated ear.
'They'll all get in a lather,'
she sighed.
AND THEY DID.

P. M. Dancer

PENN

THE SWIMMING DETECTIVE AND THE MISSING TEETH

One day
sitting in my office,
Matilda Murgatroyd the
famous actress walked in.
'My teef are mishing!'
she exclaimed. I took action.
I scanned gutters,
paths and parks.
Suddenly
something strange
appeared in the pond –
a duck with dentures.
I recovered them and collected
my reward, £500 and
cream quackers.

Mark Potter

WIDNES

Age 12

— RUNNER UP – UNDER 18 —

NW1 SPACE ODYSSEY

Across seven galaxies
they boldly went where no
Zargon had gone before. They
reported the incredible sights
they saw. They landed in
London in a radiant halo. Three
Zargons stepped out.
'We come in peace,' one told
the crowd. Behind the
spacecraft a native voice called,
'Right lads, clamp 'em!'

David Johnson

WALLINGTON

THE CYNIC'S OWN FAIRY TALE

'Be home by midnight!'
said the shadowy figure.
She danced with the prince,
sparkling with wit and beauty
and youth as the hours ticked
by, forgetting time, forgetting
warnings. When the clock
struck, she ran down the palace
steps, gown swirling, hair
streaming like a waterfall,
and broke her ankle.

Viv Leyland

SANDY

THE PRINCESS AND THE BAKED BEAN

Once there was a Baked Bean
who went in for a race.
He was running against the
Runner Bean and Prince Pea.
On the third lap
Runner Bean fell out of his pod
and the Baked Bean won.
He won King Broad Bean's
daughter.
The story's been and gone folks.

Sarah Heasman

LEEDS

Age 9

ONE GOOD TURN DESERVES ANOTHER

Once upon a time there was a
wicked witch. One day she
made a spelling mistake and
turned into a beautiful princess.
Unfortunately princesses cannot
make spells so she had to stay a
princess. She spent her life
searching for a handsome prince.
There were 3,000,000 frogs
in the land.

B. T. Inman

LAUNCESTON

MOON MUNCH

The spaceship blasted
to the moon. When it got
there the spacemen climbed
down the ladder and went off to
explore. They both went
together for fear of getting lost.
Soon the men felt hungry.
So they ate a piece of the moon,
for it was indeed
made of cheese.

Rachel Pettit

BOTTISHAM

Age 10

A MODERN FAIRY TALE

A princess was born.
Twelve fairies brought
their gifts: designer clothes,
Filofax, and compact discs.
The thirteenth fairy foretold
death by needle.
The princess ignored the
warning. At parties she drank
and smoked and shared drugs
with her friends.
She sleeps now,
waiting for a lover
too scared to kiss.

Jill Statham

WOLVERHAMPTON

SEE NO EVIL, HEAR NO EVIL, SPEAK NO EVIL

In desperate need of conversation
Arthur approached the oriental
princess. Gently and with
exquisitely composed motions
she indicated her inability to
talk, having been mute since
birth. Seizing the manual of
hand semaphore nearby he
feverishly translated
her communication.
'Guards,' it read,
'take this man out
and remove his
tongue!'

Chris Phillips

BATH

STATUS REPORT
CRAFT # 391:
SUBJECT EARTH

Intelligent lifeform smaller than
anticipated and extremely
delicate. They are in the early
stages of development, but
unfortunately have stumbled
upon nuclear physics. Global
self-destruction imminent;
re-industrialization, several
hundred years hence. They
are an unimportant species,
and pose no immediate
threat save to themselves.
Suggest we ignore.
Over.

John Kirkbride

SCOUTHEAD

THE ENCHANTING STRANGER

He
stopped
the car
and she
got in
beside him.
Moving off,
'What do you do?'
he asked. 'I am a
Witch,' she replied.
'I do not believe it;
cast a spell on me,' he
challenged. She turned
towards him with a bewitching
smile. He immediately turned
into a lay-by!

Dr R. McV. Graham-Pole

PENRITH

PAGES FROM
HISTORY

HOW THE GREATEST MYSTERY ON EARTH WAS FINALLY RESOLVED

The Gods were nervous.
They examined the standing
stones, monoliths and megaliths
scattered across Earth.
Satisfied, the Chief pushed the
first stone. With a roar of
excitement they watched the
line of collapsing stones race
around the Globe.
'It's great,' said one afterwards,
'but it takes ages to set up.'

Jenny Cameron

BRINKWORTH

THE HISTORY OF THE WORLD AS A SET MENU

Spare Ribs, Forbidden Fruit and
Eve's Pudding with God Swill.
Alternatively, there's the Big
Banger with Chicken or Egg.
'Waiter, there are Fish in my
Chemical Soup.'
Ices with Diner Sauce next.
Then, after ages and ages,
everyone's dying for bigger
pieces of the pie.
Fission Chips. Bombe.
Just Desserts.

Victoria Shearer

TALGARTH

— *RUNNER UP – ADULT* —

A BETTER PLACE

We're going to a better place,
me, Abraham and our children.
I crowded in this train but that
doesn't matter, we're going to a
better place but first we have to
shower. Only once they were in
the showers did they realise
they really were going to
a better place.

Brett Lovell

HIGHAM FERRER

Age 14

A MATTER OF OPINION

From sunny peace I was taken
into hell's mouth. Manacled,
starved, beaten and left; rich
cargo. My good man and my
sweet babies dragged from my
outstretched arms, lost forever.
On arrival, the dead were tossed
aside, the living set to work.
'Slave woman', said Missis, 'we
shall civilise you.'

Kay Mooney

SOUTH WOODHAM FERRERS

BEAU BRUMMEL RIDES AGAIN

My hypnotist had only just
regressed me into my former
life when a massive stroke
precipitated his next.
These clothes are more flashy
than convenient and toilet
facilities less than adequate, but
I've turned the situation to
financial advantage at least.
I am teaching my fat friend
the Prince Regent contract
bridge.

Dr G. M. Jolly

CARLISLE

THE ELECTRIC LIGHT BULB

The click of a switch
and in a corner a light
bulb flickers. The room is no
longer in total darkness.
Shadows move around, looming
over you. Highlights on objects
give a shiny unreal look. Your
eyes adjust to the sudden
brightness. The invention of
electricity has changed
our world.

Nicholas Evans

ASHTEAD

Age 11

THE EAGLE AND THE SPHINX

A man stands on the Pharaoh's
creature as the sun sets over the
red river. A millenium and
more before, another had
stood there.
The great soldier's eagle,
bloodied after great battles for
a far away land, was lost in
the earth. The other had
found it. His name,
Napoleon.

Gavin Falconer

GLASGOW

Under 18

HESS

1987, and Peace Talks in
Geneva.
He was pacing very slowly: years
had passed beyond his prison
walls.
'Good morning,' said a
guard. The prisoner gave no
answer. In his skull rattled the
phantasms of the century.
Later, as darkness fell, he spoke.
'Is Adolf still alive? Did we
win?'

Brian Aldiss

— *COMMISSIONED EXAMPLE* —

SHELF HELP

'It is indeed imperative that the hypotenuse cosine equates to the load bearing equilibrium of this structure as I have proved logarithmically,' postulated the great mathematician. 'Coupled,' rejoined the celebrated artist, 'with harmonious conceptual aestheticism.' 'Please,' said Mrs. Archimedes, 'who is actually going to put up my kitchen shelves?'

Annabel Scott

SURBITON

INGRATITUDE OR REVENGE?

I lived in Nairobi and played
golf. Gilbert was my regular
caddie and we came to like and
respect each other.
I had Gilbert
educated
and he rose
in Government
Service. We played
golf together but he never won.
Now I am ruined.
Gilbert has not renewed
my work permit.

R. H. Parry

ASCOT

NOTHING IS PERFECT, OR IS IT?

It was designed to cause
widespread destruction.
It was manufactured in dispersed
factories.
It was assembled by skilled
German workers.
It was delivered by dedicated
Luftwaffe pilots.
It was a parachute mine.
It was dropped on my Nissen
hut.
It was faulty.
It was a lucky night.
It was perfect.

E. Hitchcock

ETCHINGHILL

LOVE AND
MARRIAGE

A PROPOSAL

She studied his face;
an acceptable face, she thought,
with mutton-chop whiskers
fringing a rather rounded
intelligent phiz.
Her mind wandered.
She visualized vast concert halls,
pristine steam yachts, statues,
docks, museums, public houses,
regiments, mountains, glaciers,
battleships – and watch chains.
She smiled.
'Marry me, Albert,'
said the Queen.

George F. Swaine

HASSOCKS

THE MARRIAGE

John was a happy young man
and had good reason to be.
Had excellent health,
looks and an active brain.
Had everything that anyone
could wish for except one thing.
Pursuing this elusive state, John
lost all his other precious
attributes.
For it is not a word,
but a sentence.

Simon Pepin

BOURNEMOUTH

Under 18

— RUNNER UP – UNDER 18 —

99

20 PER CENT OF
MARRIED MEN
DO . . .

'ONLY 20 PER CENT OF
MARRIED MEN DIVORCE
AND MARRY THEIR
MISTRESSES,' the magazine
article revealed.
'Rubbish!' she argued out
loud with confidence.
Eight days since he had called
her. Probably called away on a
business trip. Perhaps he was
ill? 20 per cent of her believed
that, 80 per cent knew
differently . . .

Maggie Adamson

LONDON

HOW AN IMPULSIVE PURCHASE LED TO MARRIAGE AND DISILLUSIONMENT

'What a ghastly mistake!' She gloomily surveyed her new orange dress but decided to wear it to the Fête, where it attracted the attention of a bright young man.
Years later, thinking about her unhappy marriage whilst turning out old clothes she came across the dress. 'What a ghastly mistake!'

C. J. Linzey

ASHFORD

OLD BOY NET

Jasmine Haute was having an
affair with Donald Lugg.
Ernest Haute 'phoned Donald.
Called him a rotten bounder.
Then he switched on the news.
'Hold on,' he cried. 'Shares are
down.' Became thoughtful.
Lugg was always giving her
diamonds.
Winchester, Harrow prevailed.
Jasmine Haute now Jasmine
Lugg.
Diamonds are forever!

K. Moss

BATH

WORTH THE WAIT

Now that Mrs Rivet and Mr
Grummit were married they
could look at one another naked.
Nobody could tell them off and
say 'That's a dirty thing to do.
You should be ashamed of
yourselves!' So they got into the
same bed with a torch and had a
good look.

Ivor Cutler

WHITE WEDDING

My bride's family were crying:
mine simply looked glum. Had
we the right to make them
unhappy?
'Do you take this woman . . .?'
said the priest.
I looked at Sue radiant and
brave. Her eyes said:
'I love you.'
So I took her small white hand
in my large black one.

Alice Crotch

ORPINGTON

MARITAL TRUST

His frenzied fingers
tore at the flimsy garments,
blouse, skirt — damn,
there was a slip — and
tights too. Bra and pants
dropped easily. 'Oh God, if my
wife finds out . . .' His wife's
voice made him jump;
'You're not to be
trusted even to bring
in the washing when it rains.'

C. J. L. Bowes

HARROGATE

DOWN TO EARTH

He jumped.
What exhilaration!
There was only one thing
better, and he would be busy
at that tonight with Amanda.
Janet suspected nothing. Good
old Janet, so good at so much
else, running a comfortable
home, even packing
his parachute.
He pulled the
ripcord. It
came away
in his
hand.

Brian Tucker

SAFFRON WALDEN

DYING FOR LOVE
SHE DIED IN VAIN

She married at 18 and gained
weight annually. Ten years later
he said she was fat. Hungry for
affection she dieted. Her
decrease in weight brought
no increase in attention.
Still love-starved she
died anorexic. Ever
comforted by his
substantial
sweetheart,
his loss was
never too
heavy to
bear.

Helen Riding

DIDSBURY

GRANDMAMMA'S STORY OF HOW HER FATHER MARRIED HER MOTHER IN 1861

Exams passed, Leonard set out
to request Theresa's hand.
At the inn, he met his best
friend, who confided: 'I intend
to propose to Theresa!'
Leonard said nothing, but
arrived first and was accepted.
Told years later, she said: 'I had
always loved only you!'
But did he do right?

*My grandmamma offered this true story to a
newspaper eighty years ago, without revealing
that it concerned her own parents. It was
rejected.*

Thomas Braun (The Dean)
MERTON COLLEGE, OXFORD

EARNING ONE'S CRUST

MRS BAILEY'S GLASSES

My teacher Mrs Bailey
wears a pair of spectacles.
They're rather rounded and
perched there,
glaring at you!
One day they fell!
She perched them on again.
The left lens said,
'I hate looking at books,
I want holidays in the sun.'
Mrs Bailey only sees half
the class, now.

Katy Owen

LAKE SIDE

Age 9½

COLD CALLING

Would she remember him?
Did she still live here?
Five years is a long time.
Had she changed?
He had.
The Cardin suit
and Gucci moccasins
far removed from faded jeans
and trainer shoes.
Nervously he rang the bell.
'I told you five years ago,
I don't want double glazing!'

John Reeves

FRIZINGHALL

ALL THE WORLD IS MANY STAGES

Twenty years
Jones crawled around swatting
flies for Magimeat.
They mechanised and he was
sacked.
Apathetic and penniless, he
pondered life's meaninglessness.
Breeding resistent flies became
his only relief.
Eventually the Ultra Violet
Machines bought his special flies
for research and he became
wealthy. For himself, he took
flying lessons.

M.D.J. Huygins

BRISTOL

SHATTERED DREAMS AND FALSE DAWNS

Another dawn. The frosty walk
to the front line, heart
pounding, chest tight. He
stands exposed, awaiting the
inevitable onslaught. The first
missiles whistle overhead. The
enemy's roar rises to a
crescendo. He must counter-
attack, already knowing the
futility and tasting defeat.
'Alright 3C, settle down, let's
have some quiet!'

Alan Herbert

GOLBORNE

THE INTERROGATION

'What's your occupation?'
'I am a teacher.'
'Whom and what do you teach?'
'I teach people to shoot.'
Mental note – may be useful.
'Next.'
'What's your occupation?'
'I educate people.'
Another bloody intellectual.
'What's the difference?'
'I show them where to point
the gun.'
Dangerous.
The guards took him away.

D. Wilby

HAY-ON-WYE

114

A TRUE STORY

One night some official phoned
me: 'Your brother can leave
now, Sir . . . but come by car,
he's still shaky.'
Broken and disfigured by his
injuries, Miguel fell into my
arms.
Then the official asked for
money. Well . . . it's a rotten
job.
Besides he might have to torture
me one day.

*This is based on an incident reported to me in
the late seventies, when I was coordinator for
Amnesty International work on a certain country
in Latin America.*

Alan Grounds

LONDON

THE GUIDE DOG

I take her out,
I stay with her,
I help her cross the road.
I love her and she loves me,
she kisses me good night.
Where she goes, I go too,
I'm always by her side.
I must be there,
I have to be.
I am her only sight.

Adele Brown

THETFORD

Age 15

JENNY

It was a quiet office until Jenny
came. Her endless mindless
chatter drove us crazy. When
she went it was so peaceful, just
like before, except we don't use
that old basement room now,
with the heavy iron door. Not
since we sent Jenny down there,
to find some papers . . .

Mary E. Fielder

BURNT OAK

BO-PEEP REVISITED (NORTH WALES OCTOBER 1987)

Her job is easy now,
despite the recent ups and
downs.
Eighteen months ago they
slaughtered her flock.
'Unfit for human consumption,'
they said. Redundant for
a while, she now tends the
new sheep.
They no longer wag their tails
but at least she can see them
in the dark.

Sandra Gidley

ROMSEY

FOR ART'S SAKE

A GLIMPSE OF IMMORTALITY

Before my grandfather died, he
spent a vast sum on a lifelike
portrait. It was his way of
ensuring some immortality, he
said. Propped high on pillows,
his every wrinkle was painted
exactly. We found immortality
too ugly for the wall and keep it
in the loft nearer to heaven.

Rob Shearman

HORLEY

Under 18

FOR WANT OF AN EAR

Rupert's paintings did not sell
well. Critics said the style was
inappropriate. The bank said an
advance was inappropriate.
Despairing, Rupert drank
turpentine and paint and
expired. That was last year. This
year the critics discovered him
and the bank bought a Rupert
self-portrait to hang in the
loans department.

Gerry Brownlie

SHIPLEY

THE SINS OF WAGES

Two chicks from the sticks
get into pics,
On the screen its high kicks but
at heart they're just hicks.
The brunette gets four
husbands, the blonde gets
through six,
They still feel deprived so it's
coke and a fix, Which we all
know makes a fatal mix.
So Nix.

V. J. Knight

EAST SHEEN

THE ONLY
PROVISIONAL ART

Picking up his cap,
emptying coppers into pocket,
turning for an instant to
admire his work, then
joining the herd of people.
The rain came, smearing her
eyes, her mouth turning down
at the corners, now she is
six more paving slabs.
An artist's dream
not shattered,
but faded away.

Marc Townsend

NORWICH

Under 18

THE UNKINDEST
CUT OF ALL

'The part's yours, love. Start on
Tuesday,' said the director. I
had just auditioned for the part
of Long John Silver in the new
production of *Treasure Island* by
the de Sade Theatre of the
Macabre.
'Tuesday?' I asked, 'why not
Monday?' 'On Monday, ducky,
we take your leg off.'

Jack Union

BRIGHTON

IN HONOUR OF PICASSO

They stood before the picture,
with fingers cocked around their
sherry glasses, viewing the
image with knowing, critical
admiration. Heads tilting up
and down, side to side; but alas
they did not understand, though
they pretended well to one
another. The funny thing – nor
did I, and I was the artist.

Rachel R. Lewis

TOTNES

ENIGMA VARIATION

With a feeling
of apprehension she
dialed the doctor's number.
An efficient voice answered.
'Your pregnancy test?
It was negative.'
The caller murmured her thanks
and gently replaced the receiver.
Then, gathering her skirts
about her, the Mona Lisa
stepped back into
her picture frame,
resumed her pose,
and smiled.

Mary Brook

HIGH WYCOMBE

AN AUDITION

He'd
seen twelve
violinists in the
past hour. All had been
mediocre. 'Send in the last
man,' he shouted. A small
figure, dark and wrinkled
as a walnut, entered.
The violin he clutched was
ancient. His bow-hand
was bandaged.
Smiling, he began to play.
He was easily the worst.

D.C. Godfrey

TWICKENHAM

— *RUNNER UP – ADULT* —

DONIZETTI'S OPERA TELLS EUROPE THE HISTORY OF QUEEN ELIZABETH AND MARY QUEEN OF SCOTS

Elizabeth (*sotto voce*):
Shall I kill cousin Mary?
I really don't like her.
Leicester: Try meeting her.
She's charming.
Elizabeth agrees. They meet.
Mary (to Elizabeth):
You painted bastard!
Elizabeth: I knew I didn't
like her. I'll take her head off!
Tutti: Oh look! Elizabeth is
taking Mary's head off!

Robert Fenwick Elliott

LONDON

WEALTHY MERCHANT IS HORRIFIED AT UNVEILING OF HIS WIFE'S PORTRAIT COMMISSIONED FROM RENOWNED FOREIGN ARTIST

The quality of
the painting could not
be denied, but why was
an unmistakably male
hand protruding from the
top of her dress?
Crestfallen,
the painter explains:
'You wished me to paint
her with sympathy.
Not understanding this word,
I look him up — it say
"fellow feeling in the bosom."'

R. B. N. Collins

WINSCOMBE

FRUSTRATION

The artist was excited.
Painstaking hours of description
spent on the draped sheet were
almost over. The final creases
could wait for morning light.
Eagerly he returned to his room.
A neatly folded white square lay
on the model's stool with a note
from the cleaning lady propped
on top.

Emma Brooke

LONDON

ORIGINS

The weary sculptor
wiped his brow. He had
toiled for many days, placing
a green mountain here and a
sparkling river there.
Lovingly he had moulded earth
into bone and inflated
lifeless lungs. Finally
he sprayed on feelings of
love, patience and joy.
His hands slipped
when he added hate.

Helen Brimacombe

ST SAVIOUR

Age 11

THREE FOR TIME

The
instrument
he
held
felt
so — feminine.
'Interested sir?'
He took the offered
bow and for three whole
minutes pure tender
sound filled the
auction room
otherwise
grown silent.
'Right out of my
reach, I'm afraid.'
But, just once, he
had played the only
violin he had ever
really wanted.

C. C. Bourke-Jones

SHERBOURNE

WAR AND PEACE

FAIRNESS

And the little one said,
'Roll over, roll over,' so they
took a democratic vote and the
motion was passed 9 votes to 1.
So they all rolled over and the
unpopular one fell out. And
democracy triumphed, because
democracy's good. And
everyone was happy but one,
who was dead.

Joe Healey

WINCHESTER

Under 18

WORDS THAT MOVE
THE WORLD

The prophet spoke words
of great eloquence moving his
audience who went away and
forgot. The Messiah spoke but
many wouldn't believe and were
not moved. Archimedes said he
could do it with a lever but
didn't. At last came the words
'Press the button General' and
the world moved.

Searle Siemssen

CROWTHORNE

A TRUE TALE OF INTERNATIONAL CAMARADERIE FROM A TIME BEFORE GLASNOST

In a packed Tanzanian hotel bar,
two London businessmen
introduced themselves to the
only other Caucasian present.
'I'm Ray, I'm English,' said
one. 'Jack here is Irish.'
'I'm Sergei, I'm Russian.'
The Englishman said jovially,
'Then we're almost neighbours?'
'Yes,' said the Russian bleakly,
'We are just four minutes apart!'

Sue Eddington

CRANBROOK

WHAT GOD HAS JOINED TOGETHER – MAN CAN PUT ASUNDER

On the fifth day of rioting,
God intervened. Black, white
and yellow were now but three
options in a whole spectrum of
possibilities.
Rainbow people – overnight.
On the sixth day harmony rode
abroad.
On the seventh, a small blue
publican put up a sign –
'Primary colours only – no
secondaries allowed'.

Richard J. Sayer

SWINDON

THE LOST WAR

His rule
was coming to
an end. His wife
was their prisoner,
his fortresses had fallen,
and his army was in disarray.
His palace was completely
surrounded and, except for
a few faithful servants,
he was alone. What could
be done? I tried an
escape route.
'Checkmate!'
a voice
said.

William Gibson

REDHILL

THE MODERN TYRANT

A
certain
tyrant issued
a decree proclaiming
his own unparalleled
importance. A prophet
took him to the foot of
the country's highest mountain.
'How do you feel?' the prophet
asked. 'Very small.' 'Then
repent.' Next day the
tyrant sent a team
of slaves to level
the mountain,
rock by
rock.

Ian Kitchen

TUNBRIDGE WELLS

THE GREAT BRITISH INSTITUTION – THAT IS CLEARLY STRAINED OF INTERNATIONAL PREJUDICE

The Brown Brazilian accused the
Indian and Sri Lankan of being
pale and weak. The Indian said
the chocolate-coloured South
American needed sweetening to
be tolerated.
The Yellow Chinaman said the
Brazilian kept people awake.
The Sri Lankan thought he'd be
popular any time.
It's always time for tea.

Mary Thomas

RUISLIP

TIMES NOW AND
TO COME

OUT OF THE MOUTHS OF BABES?

'Come and meet my friend on
Sports Day, Mummy.'
Sports Day came.
'Where's your new friend, Paul?'
'He's sitting on the front
bench.'
There were ten on the front
bench.
'He's wearing red shorts.'
There were three boys with
red shorts.
'His hair's curly.'
'Oh, the black one,'
said Mummy.

Kathryn Clarke

TUPSLEY

Age 15

— *1ST PRIZE – UNDER 18* —

THE JOURNEYPERSON

June rain
on windscreen, wipers sweep.
Steering strange, starts to slew
from side to side.
Hard shoulder halt, summer
skirt soaked.
Unfamiliar jack, rusted nuts; the
wheel-brace slips, knuckles
skinned. Balding spare with not
much air.
Back *en route*, heater blowing on
soggy fashion shoes.
But getting there
independently.

John Coller

MANCHESTER

WHEN THE DEVIL DID NOT COME IN DISGUISE AND NO-ONE RECOGNISED HIM

Nelson boasted of stripping
assets and throwing people out
of work. He thought my outfit
realistic, especially the horns.
A drunken gorilla cheerfully
explained how to fiddle tax
returns and pulled my tail. It's
funny how they only confide in
me at this sort of gathering.
The devil knows why.

David A. Watt

GARELOCHHEAD

144

THE FIRST SIGNS OF A LEAK IN HUMANITY

Instead of the usual ten, he
drew five buckets from the well
that morning – just enough for
his family to drink. It sparkled
faintly – his children exclaimed
in awe and wonder.
The pipes from the underground
river start to crack.
His children start to fade –
glowing.
The well runs dry . . .

Joanna Scott

STOWMARKET

Age 15

THE EYE OF A NEEDLE

Today's man said to a woman,
    'I don't need a wife.
I have a house; I can sleep
with many women; father
children; change nappies;
clean, shop and cook.'
Pride burst his buttons.
'What do I do now?' he asked.
    'Sew them on,'
    said the woman.
        Desperate,
    he married her.

P. Busk

POOLE

THINGS THEY CLAIMED

They claimed it was the latest,
the newest version out; very
modern. They said it was the
best that money could buy.
They said that it was foolproof,
waterproof, shockproof,
childproof; absolutely
indestructible. They told us it
was completely reliable. But we
had to take it back.
It didn't work.

Elizabeth Syed

CHELTENHAM

Age 14

THE PITFALLS OF A ONE TRACK MIND

Innocent, he asked,
'Dad what is vice?'
Full of exploits from the popular
press Dad gave his graphic
accounts.
'It's like this son . . .' he said,
and tried to edit the doubtful
deeds of sinful man.
'Oh,' said his son, 'I only asked
'cause I've become Vice Captain
of my class.'

Leoni Hudson

SIDMOUTH

THE SPACE CAGE

Two saddened golden orbs
watch greater orbs outside the
glass. Fired from earth, in
harness bound and wired for
sound. A monkey's paw seeks
freedom, twitching, writhing,
switching, wondering. Amusing
sightseers, alarming scientists
who monitor its antics.
Returned to earth to vivisection
then freedom in God's infinite
space. Monkey business.

A. A. Parkin

ST LEONARDS ON SEA

MISSING THE JOY OF THE MOMENT, PURSUING BEAUTY WHICH, AFTER ALL, IS ONLY SKIN DEEP.

She lusted passionately after the
diamonds; drove her doting
husband remorselessly to
acquire this one more
glittering proof
of his adoration.
Wore them to
the party,
sure they
tempered her
tarnished, faded
beauty. Placed opposite
a sparkling, flawless, white
robed nymph. Sold all her
jewels to buy a face lift.

Ann Sampson

ILFRACOMBE

150

THATCHERISM –
THE FINAL
SOLUTION

Ingenious.
Individual choice
must be paramount. With
growing confidence, she
legalised hard drugs.
Prices fell sharply.
Legitimate outlets replaced
bankrupt drug syndicates.
Crime figures plunged.
Crematorium shares surged.
City populations thinned
as the weak-spirited
succumbed. Unemployment
vanished. Only the worthiest
survived. Nobody could
complain. The unfit died
of freedom.

Vincent Hill

LONDON

— RUNNER UP – ADULT —

SUFFER LITTLE . . .

A cash conscious society was
closing the children's cancer
ward.
In a bed nearby, her elderly,
wealthy, brother lay, terminally
ill, supported by the elixir of
expensive, modern technology.
She, in failing health, would
make her statement. She
swallowed the last pill and four
score years and ten became
eternity.

R. Drinkwater

EXMOUTH

AFTER SELLAFIELD

'It was called "Sellafield"
before it was burnt up
years ago,' said Jim,
pointing to distant ruins.
'My Gran said always keep
away, because of radioactivity.
She had ten fingers,' he added,
conversationally.
'What's "radioactivity"?'
asked Igor.
'No idea,' said Jim,
as they trotted off on their
six little legs.

V. McEwan

WALLASEY

IS THE GRASS ALWAYS GREENER ON THE OTHER SIDE?

Tim was unhappy pale as snow.
Sam was unhappy dark as night.
'I want to be black.'
'I want to be white.'
Colour changed.
Job changed.
Friends changed.
Attitudes changed.
Sam was unhappy pale as snow.
Tim was unhappy dark as night.
The grass was not green, black
or white.

Heidi Holland

BEXLEY

Under 18

ANIMAL TAILS

BUTTERFLY

Tommy searched the bluebelled
wood for the wonder that
zigzagged across the jigsaw sky.
'You can catch the whole world
in that net,' grandfather said.
Suddenly it was in the net,
the jar, and home to gas,
cork and pin.
Tommy's magnified eye looked,
and saw the coloured splendour's
tears.

Brandon Clark

RICHMOND

'POLYHISTORY' – OR THE PARROT THAT HAD THE LAST WORD

Would it talk?
The man at the Pet Shop
said it would.
'Give it a new cage' –
not a word.
'Give it a swing to play on' –
not a word.
'Give it a mirror for company' –
still not a word.
One day at last the parrot spoke
'Seed'!! . . . and died!

J. P. Holland

SKELMERSDALE

SIRIUS MOONLIGHT

When we were alone
she called me baby.
She was the most beautiful
woman in Paris and she only
had eyes for me.
Each evening we would sit on
the Left Bank wishing on some
distant star.
Afterwards, she would slip
on my collar and lead and
walk me home.

Clive Gardner

ASHFORD

THE PRIZE

Redundancy hadn't knocked the stuffing out of Joe. From farm labourer owning one cow, he turned to taxidermy. He needed an arctic tern to make his collection complete, win the £50,000 'Taxidermist of the Year'.
Bill gave a tern, Joe paid with the cow. One good tern deserved an udder.

R. M. J. Williams

HOYLAKE

NEED AND DESIRE, OR IF THE PELT FITS . . .

Wealthy man stood
on his polar bear rug,
wishing it was a flying carpet.
Magically, the rug swept him
beyond the Arctic Circle where
it metamorphosed back into a
bear. Wealthy man died in
one crushing blow. Bear
appreciated the meat,
but found little
use for the strange
tweed pelt.

Chris d'Lacey

LEICESTER

CONVERTED

The
lion gazed
dreamily at its
cut paw. What a nice
man, that missionary, who,
on hearing the moans, had
fearlessly come over and pulled
out the thorn. The lion smiled
lazily as it licked the
missionary's boots – a
little tough, perhaps,
but the rest had
certainly been
very tender.

Jack Union

ROTTINGDEAN

THE TRUMPETER

He was born
with a long nose,
big feet and protruding ears.
His mother loved him.
Intelligent, with retentive
memory, he learned quickly.
Instinct led him to
become a trumpeter.
He simply must.
Was terrific.
Afterwards
he took over the herd
and all the lady elephants
thought he was
wonderful.

M. Gasecka

LONDON

CROCODILE TEARS

She loved her leopard
coat, silver fox stole and
snake skin accessories.
Then she married a naturalist
and became a fervent
conservationist enthusing
over rare species.
When, on safari, he was
eaten by a crocodile, old
habits died hard.
Now his memory lives on
in her crocodile
shoes and handbag.

D. Cockerill

ABINGDON

THE AQUARIUM

Through the glass he watched
the exotic creatures, moving
effortlessly, silently in their
world. Such beautiful colours,
how peaceful they looked. He
was glad they were there, but
pitied them – what a
meaningless existence!
He was satisfied with *his* life
though – an Angel fish in the
foyer of Lucie Clayton's.

D. C. Godfrey

TWICKENHAM

POLYGON

On Monday he moved in.
Impressed by his fluency she
welcomed him. By Tuesday the
verbosity palled. Disenchanted
she suffered a Wednesday of
constant prattle. Thursday saw
the resolve. Eviction impossible
she hatched a plan. Concussion
considered she eyed the swing.
Friday is silent. Tail feathers
litter the sandpaper.

Carol Islip

HARROGATE

FULFILLED INSIDE HIMSELF, HE BROUGHT FULFILMENT TO OTHERS – FIRST OUTSIDE THEN INSIDE FOR GOOD

Simon the Chimpanzee lived contentedly in the Royal Zoo. He particularly enjoyed the magnificent meal service. One night, self-righteous men stole Simon away. Triumphantly, they released him in the jungle. Simon approached the king of that domain to enquire about feeding times. The lion replied by swallowing him whole.

Gerry Brownlie

SHIPLEY

WHO CARES OR LAWSON'S LAMENT

Golden plovers
flew over the moor
until it was ploughed up
and planted with trees.
The trees grew into a dark
empty forest; they were then cut
down and pulped into paper.
The paper was turned into
BP applications
that nobody wanted.
No golden plovers
fly over the moor today.

E.G. Cash

LOUGHTON

HOW PANTAGRUEL, ARMED ONLY WITH A FURLED PERIODICAL, SLEW THE GREAT BLOWFLY IN THE BOUDOIR

Oh,
the buzzing
and the flitting
and the waiting
and the crouching
and the leaping
and the swishing
and the missing
and the poising
and the aiming
and the thwacking
whacking whamming;
again the droning
and the mocking;
then the luring
and the feinting
and the bashing
and the
SQUASHING.

A.E. Leeding

STROUD

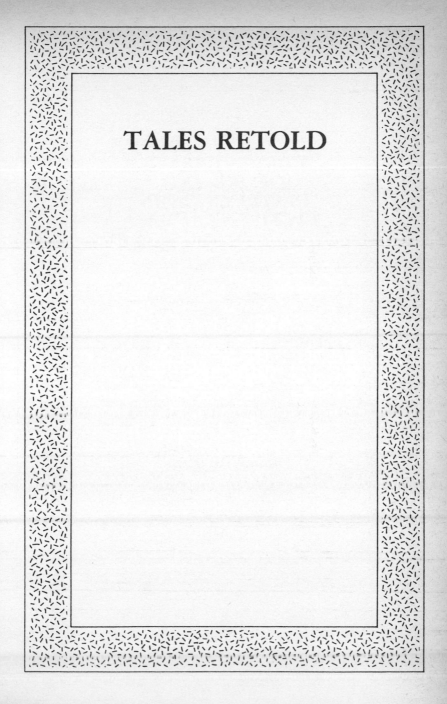

TALES RETOLD

DO COLOUR AND CURVES CREATE DESIRE AND DESTRUCTION IN TACTILE TRAUMAS?

Her curvaceous shape clad in
this season's classic taupe
palpitated at the sight of his
red, black and silver high
tech style.
Compulsion drove her to him.
Bodily entanglement exploded.
Despair replaced desire.
Damaged, unable to move, she,
the vulnerable Morris Minor,
watched him, the piratical red
Rover, speed away.

Shelagh M. Evans

COTON IN THE ELMS

THE OWL WINING AND DINING THE PUSSY-CAT

Beautiful,
giant yacht they
sailed. The bird he
said, let's wine and
dine, and got the poor
pussy-cat drunk.
He proposed on one knee
and wed her next day.
With toast as money
and tea as honey
while still in
bed, on Sunday morning.
What honeymoon could be
better?

Tracey Fairweather

THETFORD

Age 15

WHY THE FASHION INDUSTRY NEARLY WASN'T

In the almost beginning there
was Man, Woman, Subtle
Serpent and Forbidden Fruit.
'Eat!' tempted Subtle Serpent.
'Gain knowledge!' So they ate.
Suddenly they knew they were
naked and sought frantically for
aprons. But all they found was a
note from the Head Gardener —
'Sorry, sinners, fresh out of figs.'

Sir Robin MacLellan
C.B.E.

GLASGOW

HAMLET'S SUMMARILOQUY

Ghost says Uncle Claudius
poisoned regal father to reign
and marry mother. Uncle reacts
guiltily to test.
Lecturing mother Gertrude I
stab spy Polonius, girlfriend
Ophelia's father. Lamenting her
suicide, brother stabs me with
poisoned blade in duel – I him
and Claudius. Gertrude drains
my poisoned cup. All die.

Dr W. I. D. Scott

CHESTER

NEW YORK DETECTIVE

The name's Marlowe,
Marsh Marlowe.
I walked to the office that
morning, when I noticed the
light on. The door was ajar
(it was jam packed).
Inside was a beautiful doll.
She had a case for me;
but I turned it down.
Who would want a case
from a toy!

Gareth Davies

COLNE

Under 18

THE FIRST FAMILY AT HOME

They often quarrelled.
'If you had kept off the cider –
and me – we would still have a
lovely home,' she shouted.
'It's alright except for the
serpent,' he said, adding, to
their son, 'Do something to
justify your existence.'
'Yes, I'll start another trend,' he
said, glancing at baby Abel.

Edward Stocker

BRIDGWATER

REVOLUTION IN THE ENCHANTED FOREST

The girl stood at the cottage
door and waved her men off to
work – sweet guys but they
took her for granted. She had
had enough!
She needed to feel valued; to
have the self-esteem that a paid
position would give her. Snow
White packed her bags – and
left.

Faith Sutters

BEMBRIDGE, I.O.W.

CITY SAGA

'Watch it!' she cried, but her
brother was too busy judging a
beauty contest.
'Look out!' she warned, but her
father went on playing with his
soldiers and horses.
'Oh, stuff it!' said Cassandra,
and went to play with Europa's
bull; she didn't see the bear
hiding in the undergrowth.

B. L. King

BRAMPTON

SO YOU THOUGHT IT WAS A MODERN IDEA

Bravely
he rode to slay
the dragon, sunlight
gleaming on his armour.
He was not afraid. He knew
not the meaning of fear.
Reaching the dragon's lair, he
cried, 'Dragon, prepare to die,
say your prayers!'
The Dragon promptly roasted
and devoured him, crying.
'God, how I hate tinned food!'

Terence Brady

NEWCASTLE-UPON-TYNE

DEATH OF A LEGEND!

He
used to
travel around
the world and back,
and ride across the sky
with his trusty reindeer.
He climbed down chimneys
every Christmas Eve.
Then, exhausted, covered
in coal dust, he would reach
his icy home. But all this is
no more, for Father Christmas
has discovered
'Red Star'!

Karen Sartorio

BINFIELD

Under 18

OLD MYTHS RE-WRITTEN, OR MODERNISM CARRIED TO EXTREMIS

A successful writer,
he loved her untutoredness;
married her. Tutored by love,
she learnt fast; became his
secretary, wrote a bestseller.
He tried photography;
she watched, bought a camera,
gave a highly acclaimed
exhibition. He painted her
portrait – as Medusa; she
donned a snakeskin wig.
Without a shield,
he died.

Mary Hodgson

EASTHAM

WHAT HAPPENED WHEN AN OLD SEAMAN MET SOME CONTEMPORARY WEDDING GUESTS

Me and me two mates
was at this wedding
when this skinny old guy
comes up and 'angs on to me.
Gave me the willies 'e did,
talking about killing a seabird,
being becalmed
and water water everywhere.
'E won't tell nobody else though
– me and the boys mugged 'im.

Rosemary Browne

BARRY

THE REASON OF MAN AND THE INSTINCT OF THE BEAST

A woodsman lived in a cottage with his baby. By day he hewed timber, his trusted Alsatian guarding the infant. One evening he found turmoil, the cot overturned, the dog with bloodied muzzle. He shot it. A muffled whimper followed from the unharmed child. Nearby lay a dead Siberian wolf.

Jonathan Stoker

KING'S LYNN

THE TALE OF THE ALBATROSS – A BIRD'S EYE VIEW OF FATE

As an albatross, I always
excelled.
The shifting ocean was my
oyster.
Once, pure chance, I flew close
to a wild old man at sea.
His shot tore my flesh.
But pity that ancient mariner,
not me.
For, as his tale can never end,
the pain is his, not mine.

Richard Guassardo

LONDON

A HOARY OLD CHESTNUT BRIEFLY RECOUNTED

Oldest member ensconced,
otherwise nobody there. Lonely,
Adam approached: 'Whisky, sir?'
'Don't drink. Tried once.
Didn't like it!'
Mellowed, Adam regained
courage: 'Cigar?'
'Don't smoke. Tried once.
Didn't like it.'
Undeterred: 'Billiards?'
'Don't play. Tried once. Didn't
like it. But my son's due;
he'll play.'
'Your *only* son?' Adam quizzed.

Donald Alcock

REIGATE

PROBLEMS WITH
THEIR SOAP BOX

The Neighbours are complaining
because the Young Doctors
like practising in
their country.
Meanwhile
their Sons and
Daughters are cavorting
in Santa Barbara. The Sullivans'
Dynasty are claiming
originally to be Eastenders
while Howard is losing his Way,
as he comes to his Crossroads
at this point in his life.

Anna Wilders

THETFORD

Age 13

CHANGE OF PLAN

Mrs Shepherd
admonished the landlord,
'You shouldn't have let them
have the caravan!'
Cass King shrugged as
Joe burst through the
door – 'The baby's coming!'
In the lamplight from the open
doorway the animals had
gathered. Joe, the
Kings and Shepherds arrived
breathlessly.
'Oh, Joe,' said Mary,
'look – a girl!'

J. M. Jenkins

STRATFORD-UPON-AVON

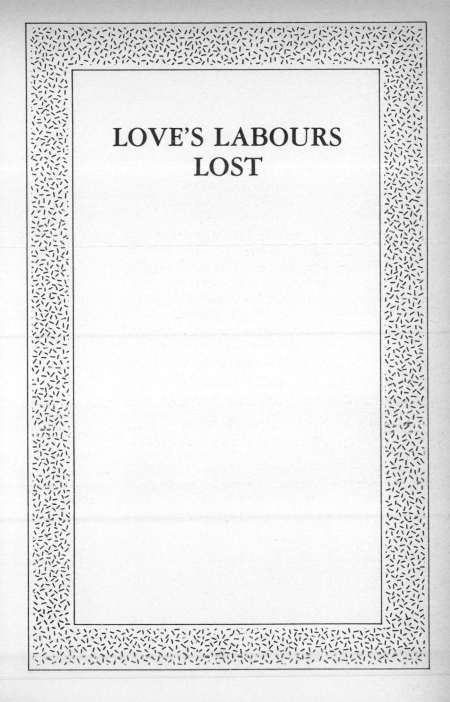

LOVE'S LABOURS
LOST

THE WILDER SHORES
OF LOVE

'What exactly
did Oscar Wilde do?'
she asked.
Because she liked plain speaking,
he answered in anatomical detail.
The air frosted with distaste and
he finished with a nervous laugh –
'Well, old queens generally carry
on like that.'
His mother rose, all dignity.
'Bertie,' she said, 'We are not
amused.'

M. H. Johnson

OXFORD

— RUNNER UP – ADULT —

188

A WARM RELATIONSHIP

'I'm cold,' she said.
She shivered and held
herself tightly.
'My love will keep you warm,'
he said with enthusiasm.
She tried his love.
'I'm still cold,' she said.
'Here's money,'
he said, disappointed.
'Go and buy yourself a fur coat.'
She smiled and warmed with a
shiver of anticipation.

Martin Russell

LEEDS

NEVER GO BACK

My first Italian holiday,
my first love, tall,
dark, handsome. Romantic,
passionate, together for ever.
'Not so,' said my parents,
'come home.'
Yes, but I'd be back and
he'd wait.
Twenty years – I went back.
There he was, fat, old. How to
escape? 'You used to be so
lovely,' he said.

Winifrede Morrison

DORKING

BLISS AND BREAK UP

They met. 'Let me share my
joys and sorrows with you,' she
said.
'Never mind the sorrow, I'll just
take joy,' said he. She smiled.
They embraced. She promised to
love, honour and be always
happy.
Time passed and sometimes her
smile slipped.
'Remember your promise,' he
said. They parted.

Diana Grant

LONDON

CHANCE ENCOUNTER

'Morning.' I know him.
'How are you?' Face familiar.
'Long time.' When?
'Fancy.' Drama group?
'Remember?' The war?
'How's the cooking?' Church?
'Keeping well?' Hospital?
'Seems like yesterday.' Gas
fitter,
'Was all for the best.' Double
glazing.
'Owe you a lot – cheerio.'
Got it. The chap Julie
ran off with.

Tony Snitter

TONBRIDGE

A LITTLE OF WHAT YOU FANCY

Spotted this skinny
women's libber in the
boozer, did old Basher.
Wooed her on a bet:
Sanders-Brahms at the
NFT, improvised equality over
lentils, bedding to Buxtehude.
She grappled him, voracious.
Laugh? A month later,
she left a pillowed note:
'Will you Ms me now I've
gone?'
Basher wept.

John Coleman

LONDON

NO HIDING PLACE

All-seeing and all-knowing,
your brittle façade crumbles
before me. I despise your
gewgaws, your vulgar chattels,
your cheap and cluttered closets.
Unheralded I come to mock
your pauper feast of beans.
You seek to assuage me with
gold, but still I know for I am
the window-cleaner.

R. L. Dyson

SHEFFIELD

CARELESS LOVE

The kettle sang from the
kitchen as she quickly tidied
round the room, occasionally
looking toward the door. Today
he would come, and there would
be laughter and talk. Her
grandson loved her stories.
The day moved on, he didn't
even phone. Three times that
week the kettle boiled dry.

Caroline Ward

READING

THE LOVE CHILD

They were born
many miles apart.
He had stumps for legs,
she had fins for arms.
At the births obstetricians
thought infanticide would be
welcomed by their parents.
Love kept them alive.
They met much later and,
as a result of their handicapped
coupling, love gave them a
perfect child.

V. M. Buckland

COLERAINE

NOTES

God how he
irritated her with
that tolerant sympathetic smile.
He turned and the light caught
the wooden spot in his pupil
where she believed he closed
himself off from the world and
her. She glanced away towards
the mirror behind
him where her eyes held
a plank expression.

*Alan and Marion
Alexander*

WHITEHAVEN

A CAUTIONARY TALE OF THE CALORIFIC PITFALLS ON THE ROAD TO TRUE LOVE

Hasn't
phoned yet.
Peanut butter
sandwich. Don't
see why I should.
Jam doughnut. Doesn't
love me anymore. Half
baguette, brie and pickled
onion. Probably out with
someone thinner. Is there
cheesecake in the freezer?
I will not phone. Just
one square of chocolate.
Ring ring. Hiya,
meet me for
dinner?

Penny Maplestone

LITTLEHAMPTON

FROM TOP TO TOE

WE'VE ALWAYS BEEN A CLOSE-KNIT FAMILY

'There's only
the two of us left now.
You've got to be grateful
to those transplant pioneers,
back in the 80s. I'd have been
dead ten years but for Ron's
lungs and Auntie Kitty's liver
and kidneys. I'll be needing
a change of heart soon.
How are you feeling,
George?'

Geraldine Cox

ELTHAM

HOLD VERY TIGHT PLEASE

She always dozed before
alighting by the hospital. He
studied her across the aisle. She
wore no ring. Desire drove him
to speak but anxiety held him
back, crushed him with the
force of a heart attack. Using
her training, she strove to
resuscitate him. Her
kiss saved his
life.

C. J. Waterman

MAIDSTONE

WRAPPED AROUND HER LITTLE FINGER

The
first
touch of
her flesh,
despite flaws,
was all he had
anticipated.
He could not tear
himself away, but
felt no pangs. He
exulted in being slave
to her will.
The healing quality
of their relationship
delighted him.
But now he dreaded
separation – as do all
strips of Elastoplast.

Roger Barrett

LONDON

A SURGEON'S TALE

Precisely,
my latex-
gloved
fingers
probe the
incision. All
trust my skill,
my experience, my
steel nerves, my
decisions, my actions.
Urgency now, as I
force myself to
look away from the
gleaming theatre clock.
Speed is the patient's
only hope. It is 63
minutes since my
last drink, precisely.

Richard Fox-Bekerman

ALDERLEY EDGE

THE AMPUTATION

We dropped a few goals together
and took a few wickets.
Together we were blown up —
escaped via Dunkirk. We stayed
together from Baghdad to
Trieste. We sailed together in
peacetime. We played with our
children. We prayed together,
we grew old together. Now
we've been parted — Goodbye
Old Friend!

Graham Castle

SALFORDS

BLIND SUMMIT

Walking along an isolated
clifftop, I encountered a stranger
gazing steadily at the
magnificent panorama.
'Wonderful to be alive; to
appreciate the colours of the sea,
the cloud shapes and the green
islands. Nature is wonderful to
behold,' I say breezily.
'Your words are my view,'
murmurs the blind stranger.

Linda Leonard

DUNDEE

ALWAYS REMEMBER WHAT WOULD HAPPEN IF YOU WERE IN AN ACCIDENT, SAYS MOTHER

Peter groaned where
he lay. Faces waved above him;
distant sirens approached.
Slowly, his memory returned.
The bus, turning, turning . . .
suddenly, terror struck him.
What did mother always, but
always, warn?
As realization dawned, a slow
smile crossed his face. Joy, oh
joy, his underwear was new
that very morning.

A. A. Rawlinson

HATFIELD PEVEREL

YOU CAN'T PLEASE
ALL THE PEOPLE ALL
THE TIME . . .

Frank had *grande mal*.
The pills gave him gumrot,
the fits worse. When the
neurosurgeon offered him new
hope, he seized the opportunity.
A something-ectomy,
it was called.
Afterwards, Frank had
two minds residing
in the same head.
His was ever so grateful,
but his friend's wasn't.

Dave Durant

BRISTOL

FOOT SAW
OR THE TALE OF
TWO FEET

We don't look forward to
luxuriating in the bath much
these days, now you are old and
fat and cannot reach over your
somewhat portly paunch. We
barely see the soap and have
only a passing acquaintance with
the loofah. We feel, and are,
neglected; please remember us –
your feet!

Pamela Broster

OADBY

KNOT WHAT YOU'D EXPECT

She wriggled into her leotard
and opened the book.
Sweating with pain and
discomfort, she struggled
valiantly to follow the diagrams.
She was progressing well — until
she realised her mistake
in not buying the second
volume. She sighed,
never mind, her ankles
would keep the back of
her neck warm.

Anon

NOTHING TO SEE

Perhaps it didn't matter that
Arthur was born blind. He
seemed happy. Aware of his
surroundings by senses other
than sight, he 'saw' things
others didn't.
For though his eyes stared
out at darkness, if he
seemed to see through
people, it was because
there was nothing
there to see.

N. Marsden

LEICESTER

THIS WORLD OR
THE NEXT

ADA'S WORLD

In Bolton, after the telegram,
Ada enshrined the neat terraced
house.
In French sanatoriums Arthur
languished for four decades;
neurasthenic, unidentified.
During the fifties modern drugs
excoriated his stygian existence.
Now they're together, at least,
in the same town; the shrine
immaculate.
Ada impenetrable, she hurries
past him, he's homeless.

Robert Gore

H M PRISON
LEYHILL

MINGLING TEARS

He was born
on the warm ashes.
She was born
amid antiseptic clatter.
He married
under the strong school tree;
she in a massive cathedral.
He sired eighteen children.
She planned two.
When her youngest died,
she sued.
When his died, he accepted
fate quietly.
They both cried deep tears.

John Thynne

KNEBWORTH PARK

SMILE THOUGH YOUR ART IS FAKING

He wasn't all there. Tactfully,
they concealed
his wellingtons. Weeds choked
the allotment.
    Grateful, he plucked the
dahlias from carpets;
offered transparent bouquets.
Disbelieved, they went
unwatered. He wilted.
    Bedfast, he captured
butterflies, exhibiting
    empty hands. Heads shook.
Leaves were taken. Tributes
feigned.
    Gone, he pushes up their
plastic roses.

Heidi Thomas

— COMMISSIONED EXAMPLE —

DISCUSSION BETWEEN CITIZEN OF THE WORLD AND SAINT PETER AS TO WHETHER ADMISSION BE GRANTED

'My Ambersons were
Magnificent.'
'Really?'
'I panicked America
over the radio.'
'Huh.'
'Rosebud?'
'Dollar-book Freud – your
description!'
'I exploited Hearst.'
'There's that.'
'Slimmed down for Falstaff.
Played him as Shakespeare's
good, pure man.'
'Persuasive.'
'Been accused of acting
omnipotent.'
'Welcome, Orson. We need all
the help we can get.'

Roy D. Outram

MEXBOROUGH

I'LL MISS YOU MUM

I'll never forget that day,
the family telling me not to
worry, be strong they said.
It was alright for them,
I mean they knew her longer
than I did
and she was so pretty.
Now what have I got,
a memory.
I want more than that,
I need her.

Sarah Marriott

HEANOR

Age 14

NO HAPPY RETURN

Tom detested birthdays.
Nobody cared it was his today.
He decided to take
that final swim.
However
a surprise party
had been planned for weeks.
Even as he laid his clothes
on the beach, glasses were raised
to him. And while they
drank his health,
Tom was drowning
his sorrows.

Steven Bonham

BRISTOL

THE TIMES – SEPTEMBER THIRTIETH OBITUARY 'AN ANONYMOUS LIFE OF DEDICATED SERVICE'

Born nineteen-thirty
near Oporto, he passed
examinations with honours.
Success meant emigration to
England where he traded
in West End.
Settled down in large country
house. There he aged,
matured and prospered.
Ultimate accolade in
vintage years.
A Royal Command performance.
EPITAPH:
'Born a grape but died a toast.'

Richard Coverley

MERSTHAM

BIOGRAPHY OF ÅSA WRIGHT, BORN 1899, ICELAND (LAND OF SAGAS); DEBUTANTE, LONDON; GRANDE DAME, TRINIDAD

Her London, remembered,
glows with gaslight, Hansoms,
handsome beaux.
Caribbean farming prospered.
Now, Spanish moss drips;
vampire bats bit the donkey.
Only Nolly, vest filthy, sweeps
the verandah.
She rests, heavily shapeless
as sodden, forgotten sacks
of cocoa pods.
Indoors, mildew dims Court
portraits of the girl with white
plumes.

Merryl Cook

STOCKPORT

WELL, I'LL BE A LOGICAL POSITIVIST!

'I thought you said there was no
heaven Bertrand, what are
you doing here?'
'Is that you Wittgenstein?' the
squeaky, pedantic voice asked.
'And who's that playing chess
with Einstein?'
'You never did recognise Him.'
'Albert looks very worried,
doesn't he ever win?'
'That's the trouble Bertie, he
never loses!'

W. Owen

LIVERPOOL

MEMOIRS OF AN ELDERLY LADY WHOSE FAVOURITE OCCUPATION WAS KNITTING

Unable to read or write, she
knitted her memories instead.
They began with plain knit in
white, continuing with purl in
pink. Intricate patterns in
bolder colours filled the middle
gradually fading to grey with a
few dropped stitches.
It was a long scarf — neatly
cast-off at the end.

Maureen Brigden

BAGSHOT

EARLY ONE MORNING

'You can get up now,' said the nurse sweetly. 'I thought I was dying, yesterday,' said old Rebecca. 'Well, you're alive today and your family are waiting for you.'
'You mean . . . my daughter and my grandchildren?' 'Not yet,' smiled the nurse, 'but look – your husband and your parents are here.'

Canon Derek Fathers

WEST KIRBY

GONE TO HELL –
BACK SHORTLY

Afterwards he knew
that it had all been
a mistake. It ought never
to have been allowed to happen.
Being born was no joke.
Growing up no pleasure.
Growing old even
worse. As he tried
to tell them. And death
when it came seemed like a
blessed release.
Until afterwards . . .

Brian Redhead

— COMMISSIONED EXAMPLE —

THE TUPPERWARE MAN

He kept
his tobacco
in a sage-green
tub with a stay-fresh
lid and ate his meals from
plastic plates and bowls,
cutting up the food with
colourful polythene cutlery.
When he died the company
honoured him with a
special product;
a lemon-yellow
coffin with a
resealable
lid.

Paul W. Nash

OXFORD

WORDSMITHS

THE PARABLE OF THE BEST SELLER

He made up a story. The critics
praised it for its sensitivity,
political comment, allegory,
moral implications, fine use of
language, and the delicate
balance of the characters.
'It was nothing really,' he said 'I
didn't mean to incorporate all
that. I just thought *The Good
Samaritan* was a catchy title.'

B. Thompson

LONDON

WORDSWORTH HALLUCINATES

I wandered lonely as a cat
That thinks it owns both
dale and hill,
When suddenly I saw a rat
The colour of a daffodil.
When next I saw a penguin pass
With scarlet chest and
tartan bill,
I just collapsed upon the grass
And knew that I was ill.

Brian Aldiss

— COMMISSIONED EXAMPLE —

COMMERCIAL VIABILITY

Consumed by consumption,
starvation, cold, a poor,
unrecognised artist dies young.
Years later, in his opulent office,
the rich publisher who bought
the lucrative rights to the dead
artist's work regrets that he
cannot sell planned works that
the artist might have completed,
had he lived.
Many more remain, penniless.

Mark Dennett

THETFORD

A Modern Fairy Tale

See no evil etc 82   81

Status report 83

Marital Truel 105

Down to earth 106

129 – Fellow feeling in the
          bosom

Out of the mouths – 142

14.3 The Journeyperson

From one character to another
                              130

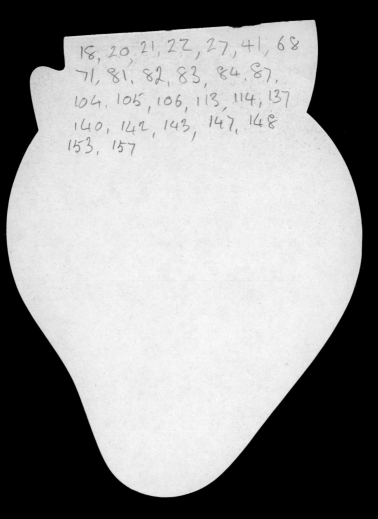

18, 20, 21, 22, 27, 41, 68
71, 81, 82, 83, 84, 87,
104, 105, 106, 113, 114, 137
140, 142, 143, 147, 148
153, 157

FILTHY RICH: THE BOOK OF THE TV MINI-SERIES

Born in poverty in Yorkshire, seduced at sixteen by a landowner, she produced both daughter and textile company alone. She grew rich, married, bore more children, founded a dynasty, alienated her family, took lovers. At eighty, she sold out to an oil sheik, began to meditate, and became a nun.

Rev. Mary Stokes

BIRMINGHAM

FROM ONE CHARACTER TO ANOTHER

Some were short and others tall,
but each complemented the
other. Most worked in groups –
some stood alone.
All vociferous in varying
degrees; a few had to be
silenced, but subsequently they
combined to make their point.
Without access to the twenty-six
of them I'd be lost for
words.

Harry Double

STOWMARKET

THE SHORTEST STORY

An English Class.
SIR said, a Short Story
must contain four principal
elements, namely,
RELIGION, SOCIETY, SEX
and MYSTERY in that order.
Write story now and
remember the four elements.
Five minutes pass,
boy puts down his pen.
SIR reads, 'MY GOD said the
DUCHESS I am PREGNANT.
WHO DUNNIT.'

J.S. Hart-Jackson

HEXHAM

IN THE BEGINNING
WAS THE WORD . . .

The white-coated
oafs here won't believe
I invented speech. In my
previous existence our hairy
tribe communicated by sounds:
'Eeeee,' 'Ooooo,' 'Aaaaa.' Then I
discovered consonants. 'G-O,' I
said suddenly. The effect was
electric! 'G-o-d,' I cried, this
time throwing in an extra
consonant. Not bad for a
beginning.

W. E. Newton

SEAFORD

WITH MURDER IN MIND

The invitation to an Agatha Christie weekend sounds fun. Twelve unhappily married couples arrive at Country House Hotel. Friday evening – 'Reception and Candlelit Dinner': *Poulet à l'Estragon* or Lamb Cutlets. Next morning there are twelve corpses and six happily widowed couples. Was it salmonella or did the butter do it?

Sue Britton

SHIPSTON-ON-STOUR

FALLING STANDARDS

They spin.
Imposed upon sheets
of white. Pictures repeated
100,000 times. The leaves
accumulate in a great wodge of
supplements, news and reviews.
They hit the streets, thumbed
a thousand times, sitting
idle upon shelves of
stores. Yesterday's
news crams our
heads, women
flaunted in tabloids,
gossip blows our minds.

Jon Wagstaff

WOKINGHAM

Age 14

THE LONG ARM OF THE PRESS

The famous
explorer and his
small party scanned
the desert anxiously.
A dusty column was
approaching. Friend or
foe? 'Load rifles!' Armed
men on camels emerged from
the dust. Their leader
advanced and addressed
the explorer:
'The *Telegraph Sunday
Magazine* wants the
exclusive story of
your expedition.
In 50 words.'

W. R. Trotter

HASLEMERE

GRAFFITI

Mindless destruction?
Useless scribble?
Some may see it as that,
but for others it is an art form,
a way to let loose their
emotions, a decorative form
of writing.
'Scrub the walls!' say some.
'Cover the bare breeze-blocks
and brighten our lives!'
say others.
Me, I don't mind.

Nicola Elkin

BARTON-UNDER-NEEDWOOD

Under 18

ET CETERA

THE CRITIC

I took it all down,
exactly as He said
and no copy-editing.
I was carrying it back for
distribution when He called
after me, 'Any comments?'
'Maybe it's a bit negative,'
I suggested.
'Come back here,' He
thundered. 'And take down
another one: "Number Eleven:
Thou Shalt Not Quibble."'

Margaret Bacon

HIGHWORTH

— *2ND PRIZE – ADULT* —

THE JOBBERNOWL

He was a child once, shouting,
'Let's pretend!' But his feet
never really left the ground. He
sought adventure without
imagination, cheap as it was.
He is an adult now, whispering,
'Let's be realistic!' But he is
sinking. He has found
imagination, yet wallows in
stagnation, costly as it is.

Kit McQuillan

LONDON

A PUPIL'S TALE –
LIFE IS NOT WHAT
IT SEEMS AT FIRST
SIGHT

She rose imperiously *ex cathedra*.
'Ronnie. My gloves.'
Convent trained she could not
    proceed without them.
As he grovelled on the ground
at her feet she could sense the
whole restaurant gasping, 'I bet
she leads him a dog's life!'
She laughed –
'You see they didn't realise I
    was blind.'

Anna M. Burns

BROADWAY

THE EXTRAORDINARY PASSPORT

Soon he must take action to
regain entry into that magical
world. A world where he could
be instantly transported
anywhere. To the vast depths of
the oceans and into the infinite
reaches of space, to travel back
and forth in time. Yes,
tomorrow he must renew his
library ticket.

Denis Connolly

FERRING

241

I'VE GOT THOSE OTHER MAN BLUES

Other man's house bigger
Other man's car faster
Other man's wife prettier
Other man's talk wittier
Other man's insults sharper
I punch other man
Other man punches harder
Other man and I in hospital
Other man's doctor cleverer
Other man's nurse leggier
Other man and I in toilet
Other man's . . .

Peter Wotton

SUNBURY ON THAMES

242

SUMMER COLOURS

Black and yellow are the
honey bees,
The rose red colour of the
scented rose trees,
The green grass glistens in the
fresh morning dew,
Delphiniums nod their heads
of blue,
The flash of pink as the linnet
flies by and
The fluffy white clouds against
the bright blue sky.

Melanie Lynch

COLCHESTER

Age 11

WHAT SHE WOULD DO FOR TWO PINS

A compulsive knitter, she
completed several hundred rows
a day. Starting with bacon rind
at breakfast and continuing with
clues unravelled from the
Telegraph crossword, she arrived
at work to knit the boss's
shoelaces, and spaghetti at
lunch. Home time would see
her wearing a new hat with
matching scarf.

M. Francis

FOLKESTONE

IT'S JUST A MATTER OF COMPARISON

Wealthy couple had twin boys in middle age, born handicapped. Decided abnormality is only comparative so bought a beautiful island and brought children up there, employing only people with similar handicap. When adult, sons arranged killing of old couple. Caused heartache, but was the kindest thing, weren't like other people.

Jennifer Lewis

BEXLEY HEATH

THE EMPIRICAL METHOD

Katanga suspected his uncle of keeping back a portion of his inheritance. But magic was hard to measure.

He caused colic in the man's goats, dried up the breasts of his youngest wife, and, finally, gave him wasting disease. Only one with witchcraft could have lingered withering for so long.

Dave Durant

BRISTOL

WHAT'S IT ALL ABOUT?

Alfie always wondered about
the meaning of life.
When his parents died, he used
his inheritance to travel the
world seeking an answer. His
quest finally brought him to an
aged Tibetan lama called
Lu Shang.
They talked. Ultimately the
truth was revealed. The old man
hadn't a clue either.

V. J. Hughes

PRITTLEWELL

ME TOO

As they approached each other
on the pavement they were
clearly heading on a collision
course.
As they got closer neither
altered course.
They collided.
'Did you not see my white
stick?' he said angrily.
She replied calmly, 'if I could
see your white stick I would not
need mine.'

L. H. Edwards

EDINBURGH

ANOTHER COMPUTER ERROR

What will she be like?
She may be grotesque, fat and
ugly. They said the computer
guaranteed a perfect match but
how does it know? I'm no oil
painting but, please God, make
her acceptable. This must be
her now. Oh no! It's even
worse than I imagined.
She's beautiful!

Brian Morrison

SHREWSBURY

— *RUNNER UP – ADULT* —

HOW THE BBC'S BOUNTY REVEALED VISTAS OF HOPE TO ONE MAN KEEPING HIM SANE

Sea
and sand
cleaned the
bowl after raw
pomfret salad. Over
years on the island his
remaining disc lost its
grooves. So he fashioned
the bowl. He sang the Bible.
Memorizing Shakespeare also,
he acted entire plays – role
by role. Prepared, if
his ship came,
to be bishop
or actor.

Sylvia Forde

LONDON

— RUNNER UP – ADULT —

250

THE LIFE OF A CHRISTMAS TREE

Here
I am standing
all alone in the snow.
Is that footsteps approaching?
A man
with an axe
cuts me down. He drags
me away to his house, puts
pretty balls on my branches and
parcels
under me. After
Christmas they throw me
away like a piece of unwanted
rubbish.

Philip Lentern

THE WEST OF ENGLAND SCHOOL
FOR CHILDREN WITH LITTLE OR NO
SIGHT

EXETER

Age 13

AM I MAD?

How long I've been here,
I know not.
I'm lonely: frightened.
Why do they conceal me from
the world? They say I'm mad.
I'm not mad, am I?
People. I envy their freedom.
I sit, waiting,
awaiting their precious liberty.
Then I snatch it. Ha! . . .
Shall I show you how?

Rita Das

AYR

Age 13

— RUNNER UP – UNDER 18 —

CHEERS!

One for the road?
Cheers!
Well, well, look who's here.
Cheers!
A quicky? Cheers!
It's my shout.
Cheers!
Ring her up and tell her,
cheers.
Heard about Marianne?
Cheers!
They said you could not recognise
the boy's body which her car hit.
A terrible thing. A large
Scotch please.
Cheers!

M. J. Taylor

OLD

CHRISTMAS MORNING

The
children
are awake; their
eyes twinkling with
anticipation. Their greedy
podgy
hands groping
to the end of the bed
with unfeeling rapaciousness.
With
illusions
of dolls, trainsets,
sweets . . . The stockings
are gleaming and special – filled
with
Gold,
Frankincense and Myrrh.
The children are full
of disappointment,
revulsion – and
rejection.

Claire Kennedy

GLASGOW

Age 14